THE SHOE TREE
of
CHAGRIN

by J. PATRICK LEWIS

illustrations by CHRIS SHEBAN

CREATIVE EDITIONS

THE
SHOE TREE
of
CHAGRIN

Text copyright © 2001 by J. Patrick Lewis   Illustrations copyright © 2001 by Chris Sheban

Published in 2001 by Creative Editions, 123 South Broad Street, Mankato, MN 56001 USA

Creative Editions is an imprint of The Creative Company. Designed by Rita Marshall

Library of Congress Cataloging-in-Publication Data

Lewis, J. Patrick. The shoe tree of Chagrin : a Christmas story / by J. Patrick Lewis.

Summary: The barn-tall old plainswoman Susannah DeClare braves deep snow and icy weather

to fulfill her promise to deliver a load of handmade shoes to Chagrin Falls, Ohio, by Christmas.

ISBN 1-56846-173-9   [1. Shoes—Fiction. 2. Christmas—Fiction. 3. Frontier and pioneer

life—Ohio—Chagrin Falls—Fiction. 4. Chagrin Falls (Ohio)—Fiction. 5.

Tall tales.] I. Title.   PZ7.L5866 Sh 2000   [Fic]—dc21   98-050908

First edition   5   4   3   2   1

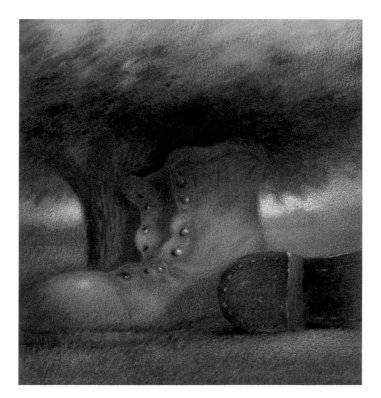

For Kelly and Scott Marceau, and for Sue, with love

J. Patrick Lewis

——

For Laura

Chris Sheban

ONCE LONG AGO, so the elders tell, the tallest of

the great plainswomen traveled the Ohio Valley in a two-wide wagon

pulled by pluck and luck and a brute horse named PawPaw, thirty-

two hands high. Susannah DeClare was as strong as a lockbox and

as long as a good spit in a windstorm. Legend told she was six feet

eight—or eight feet six—didn't matter which. Either way, to the

astonishment of townsfolk everywhere, she could reach up and scratch a cloud whenever she felt like it.

You'd often see her in the shut-eye towns of the back country, wearing old age like a gnarled oak. Was she sixty-eight? Or eighty-six? No one knew. She was at least as old as honesty, and as honey brown as the polish on her size 27 Tuesday boots. Emeralds in her eye sockets put you in mind of a wizard weaving magic with nothing more than a wink and a nod. And you always knew she was coming by the sweet rolling thunder of her song over the next rise.

Susannah DeClare made shoes with such care and fine craftsmanship that they lasted their owners a lifetime. Best work shoes, dancing shoes, showing-off shoes across ten counties and beyond.

"Shoes walk us into the wide world!" she roared. "We ought to give them back somehow—before we walk out of it."

One hot morning in the middle of June, Miss DeClare and PawPaw showed up like sunrise in Chagrin Falls, six months to the day after her last visit. The old woman set up her shingle in the town square, ready to take orders for footwear she would stitch and sew and glue as she strode hugely across the valley. It was a custom repeated in each village she visited. Six months later, she'd return to the same village again, handing out her special orders.

Wherever she went, folks clung to Miss DeClare like marmalade on toast. "Welcome back, Miss Susannah!" yelled Daniel McEldowney, craning his neck to get a fair look at her. "Did you have a tolerable winter and a prosperous spring?"

Herbert Boy Herbert leaned a ladder up against the horse's back and pitched himself on top. "PawPaw's made of soft steel!" he shouted. "Got any new adventures to tell?"

Clelia Rose tugged at the hem of the shoemaker's billowing

brown skirt. "I missed you, Lady Big!" she cried.

"We all did!" said Binny Waller, looking up in awe at the

barn-tall woman.

Miss DeClare passed out the made-to-order shoes she'd

cobbled these six months gone. Then she settled back under a shade

tree with a straw in a barrel of cider, and a smoke pipe, her bonnet

nearly hidden in the branches, and rambled on till noon about births

and deaths and weddings and all she saw from Bath to Novelty and

Orange and every post office in between.

"One thing never changes," she said, puffing like a coal stove. "Everybody cottons to fine shoes. I'll make the circuit again and hope to get back here when the snow flies. So tell me now, who would like some new DeClares by next Christmas?"

One after another the townsfolk signed up for boots and booties, sandals, hobnails and moccasins—and they paid good money gladly, knowing that Miss DeClare's word was as true as time's arrow.

For a whole year Dub Gifford had worked to save up six silver dollars in a sock to buy something very special. "If you wouldn't mind, Ma'am, a pair of shiny blue high heels, size 7, so my Ma can go dancing at the Blossom Festival. And a size 10 pair of house slippers for my Pa, 'cause he's been barefoot since New Year's."

"See what I can do, Dub," Miss DeClare nodded down at him, clinking the money in a fat purse the size of a burlap sack. Fact is, it *was* a burlap sack. "PawPaw and I'll be back in time for you to put those shoes under a Christmas tree. I promise you."

"Haw-haw-haw!" came the fake guffaw from outside the cir-

cle of gawkers. The boy who was standing there had Big City writ-

ten all over him. Reggie Kingsbury was so stuck on himself that his

two best friends were a mirror and a comb. Worst of all, Reggie didn't

believe a word about the almighty Miss DeClare and her eternity

shoes, her mile-high horse or her traveling ways. Of course, he'd

never find anything to like about somebody who stole all the shine away from his royal highmindedness, Reggie Kingsbury.

Two months earlier, he had moved to Chagrin from somewhere just west of paradise—or so he said—and he swore there were no better shoes anywhere in the true universe than the ones sold by Mr. Sears and Mr. Roebuck.

"Well, ain't you a giant eyeful! Who ever heard of Shoesannah DeClare anyway?" Reggie snorted, his haughtiness so high in the air it could have brought on nosebleed. "DeClares sounds like they oughta be apples or roses. Why, I wouldn't even be buried in a pair of 'em!" he laughed, then he lobbed an exclamation point spitteroo on the ground just to show he meant every word.

Miss DeClare unfolded her bones, stood up, gently hooked Reggie by his suspenders and lifted him four feet off the ground. "Well, son," she whispered, smooth as pudding so as not to scare the boy witless. It looked like she was wearing a beard but it was only a robin's nest that high up in a tree. "If you ever change your mind, you *could* be buried in a pair, because it's all over certain my shoes will outlast anyone."

"Put me down, Too-Tall and Terrible!" Reggie screamed. "I'll

wager my Sears tan-and-cord-i-van specials against the brand-

spankin'est new pair of shoes you'll ever make that Chagrin folks

have seen the last of you—and the last of their money, too!"

Miss DeClare set the boy down as softly as she'd picked him

up. He polished his shoes on the back of his pant legs, shuffled away as if he owned the place, and yelled back to the crowd, "Just wait and see if I ain't right." And that was the end of that.

She packed in fresh supplies, said her good-byes, drifted into the woods and then disappeared. Half a blue year's travels began all over again.

Hers was a solitary life. All her worldly goods filled the wagon—knives and nails, string and rawhide, buckets of glue, paint and shoe polish, clothes, and as much food as a heavenly body craved. In good weather, she camped out under the stars. Sometimes folks'd offer her a bushelful of greens and a night's shelter from the damp and the cold, though no bed was ever big enough to hold her. All they'd ask in return was to hear a tall tale from the endless supply she had stored away. Told true or told slant, they were plumb poetry

to listen to.

Most nights, though, alone in the woods, by the light of her

campfire and the swollen moon, she cut and hammered and molded

shoes at the rate of a dozen pairs an hour! Her only company was the

music of little night creatures. Every week or two, she and PawPaw

would mosey into the next village, where the cobbler took orders for

yet another batch of shoes.

—-—-

In late July she came to Waite Hill. A giggle

of children danced around her like she was the

big top circus come to town.

August found her among the grateful

shoe shoppers of Pepper Pike, where she fixed the

bell clapper in the church steeple on her tiptoes.

A month later, folks in Reminderville

welcomed her with a mini-parade. Miss DeClare

was the human float.

By mid-October, though, winter stood up and roared. The old woman hunkered down with PawPaw under horse blankets, but that first snow got deep into her bones somehow in a way it hadn't done before, and the fever never left her.

She'd planned to be as far as Bath by Halloween, but it wasn't to be. Cruel winds kept her stalled along the Cuyahoga River. Oh, she took a few deep breaths as usual and blew the wind back over Indiana way, but this was a season that would not be forgotten or denied.

Still, there were shoe promises to keep. So when three Indian summer days graced the river with a thaw, she ferried across at Peninsula and continued south.

By Thanksgiving, PawPaw's flanks and muzzle icicled over. He never complained. The trees of Snohio, as she called the bitter land, hung like diamond chandeliers click-clicking danger.

And still she pushed on.

But truth to tell, mighty as she was, the old cobbler woman could not outrun the years, defeat forgetfulness, or uncover the

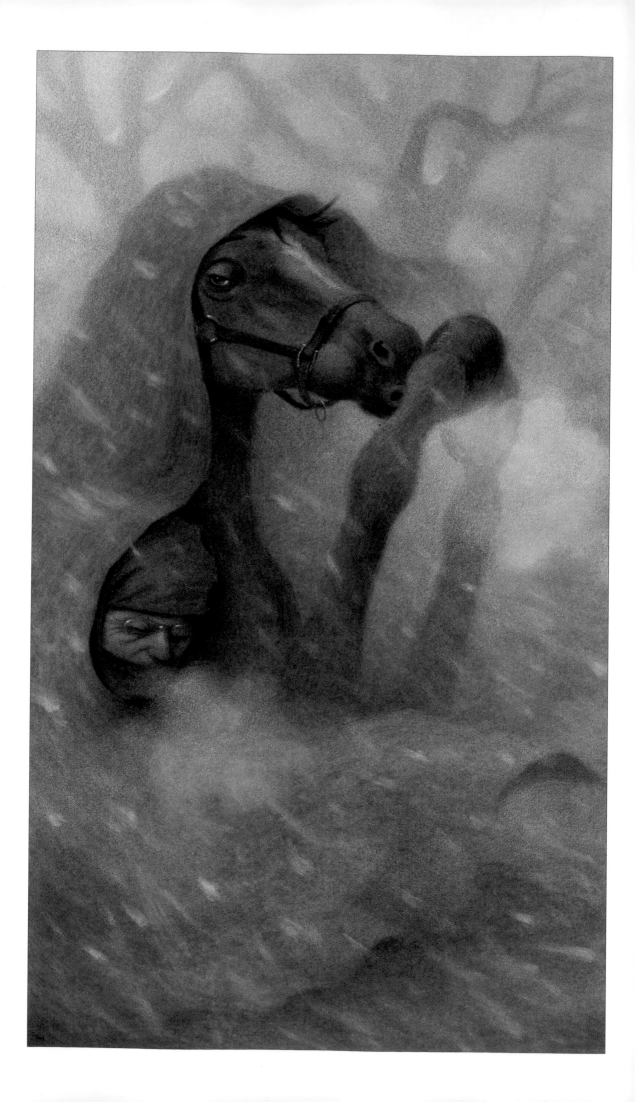

snow-blank trails, and so she fell far behind. Seven times her enormous heart skipped into oblivion, and seven times the wilds pulled her back. Two weeks before Christmas, the whole town of Bath begged her to wait out the ferocious storms. Though sick and weary, she left them in wonder and turned northeast for what would be the last time.

⚊⚊

Meanwhile, Dub, Clelia, Daniel, Herbert Boy, Binny, and a bunch of the Chagrin kids warmed themselves in Judith O'Malley's barn. As the days shortened up to Christmas, they waited for her first hill song with excitement . . . then worry . . . and finally, despair. "Where could she be?" asked Clelia Rose. "Lady Big's never been late into Chagrin!"

"I'll tell you where! Frozen stiffer than a blue spruce, that's where," offered know-it-all Reggie Kingsbury. "Or else that long

drink of water's warming her toes in a cozy inn somewheres, spendin'

your *shoe* money by the barrel!"

"Hush up, Reggie," Dub said. "She'll be here somehow." But

doubt and fear crept over Dub Gifford like window frost. Where

could she be? Maybe Reggie was right after all.

On Christmas Eve morning, a strange postcard arrived at

the Gifford cottage.

> *Dear Dub,*
>
> *The promise of Christmas*
>
> *hangs out on Savage Road*
>
> *Take the doubter with you.*
>
> *S.D.*

Shaking with excitement and curiosity, Dub was determined

to unravel the mystery. He went to each house in the village, gather-

ing small detectives as he went. Eight children set out to walk the

two miles down Savage Road, not knowing what they were looking

for or what they would find.

An hour later, near the very end of the gravel road, there it stood! Hanging from the skeleton branches of a great silver maple

were dozens of shoes made just to order—the shiny blue high heels,

the calfskin house slippers, and a pair of put-the-shoe-factory-to-

shame, black leather Sunday walkers for the doubter.

Reggie Kingsbury stood there speechless, the first time in his

life. Slowly, despite the foot-high snow, he took off his Sears specials,

hung them on a branch, and put on his new Susannah DeClares.

"Hey, what's that?" shouted Daniel McEldowney, pointing

skyward. Way up there on a branch too high to heaven hung four blue-tinted horseshoes and a pair of magnificent Tuesday boots.

Just then Dub remembered the old woman's words: "Shoes walk us through the wide world. We ought to give them back somehow before we walk out of it."

A FTERWORD

And that's exactly what folks did. Today on Savage Road in Bainbridge, Ohio, just outside of Chagrin Falls, there stands an elegant silver maple tree with a greenleaf jacket in summer, a white-ice parka in winter, and a hundred shoes the year round. Sneakers, boots, sandals, every kind of shoe you can name. If you should ever visit there, take an old shoe with you, hang it on the Shoe Tree, and make a wish...

in memory

of PawPaw and the mightiest

of the great plainswomen,

Susannah DeClare.